THE WALL

Clarion Books
a Houghton Mifflin Company imprint
215 Park Avenue South, New York, NY 10003
Text copyright © 1990 by Eve Bunting
Illustrations copyright © 1990 by Ronald Himler

Library of Congress Cataloging-in-Publication Data
Bunting, Eve, 1928-
The Wall / by Eve Bunting; illustrated by Ronald Himler.
p.   cm.
Summary: A boy and his father come from far away to visit the
Vietnam Veterans Memorial in Washington and find the name of the
boy's grandfather, who was killed in the conflict.
ISBN 0-395-51588-2
[1. Vietnam Veterans Memorial (Washington, D.C.)—Fiction.]
I. Himler, Ronald, ill.   II. Title.
PZ7.B91527WAL   1990
[E]—dc20   89-17429
                                                              CIP
                                                               AC

HOR 10 9 8 7 6 5

THE WALL

by Eve Bunting
illustrated by Ronald Himler

Clarion Books
New York

This is the wall, my grandfather's wall. On it are the names
of those killed in a war, long ago.

"Where is Grandpa's name?" I ask.

"We have to find it," Dad says.

He and I have come a long way for this and we walk
slowly, searching.

The wall is black and shiny as a mirror. In it I can see Dad and me.

I can see the bare trees behind us and the dark, flying clouds.

A man in a wheelchair stares at the names. He doesn't have legs.

I'm looking, and he sees me looking and smiles.

"Hi, son."

"Hi."

His hat is a soft, squashed green and there are medals on it. His pant legs are folded back and his shirt is a soldier's shirt.

A woman old as my grandma is hugging a man, old as my grandpa would be. They are both crying.

"Sh," he whispers. "Sh!"

Flowers and other things have been laid against the wall. There are little flags, an old teddy bear, and letters, weighted with stones so they won't blow away. Someone has left a rose with a droopy head.

"Have you found Grandpa yet?" I ask.

"No," Dad says. "There are so many names. They are listed under the years when they were killed. I've found 1967."

That's when my grandpa died.

Dad runs his fingers along the rows of print and I do, too. The letters march side by side, like rows of soldiers. They're nice and even. It's better printing than I can do. The wall is warm.

SMIT
ARNE W BEAVER ◆ JAM
OHN T DOIKE ◆ THO
AROSA Jr ◆ TERRY
S ◆ GEORGE MUNO
OBBY ROY HOLLE
ND
OHNSON ◆ THO
AME
RLES A M
T QU
AMES M
TURNE
OMP

Dad is searching and searching.
"Albert A. Jensen,
Charles Bronoski,
George Munoz," he mutters.
His fingers stop moving. "Here he is."
"My grandpa?" I ask.
Dad nods. "Your grandpa." His voice blurs. "My dad. He was just my age when he was killed."
Dad's rubbing the name, rubbing and rubbing as if he wants to wipe it away. Maybe he just wants to remember the way it feels.
He lifts me so I can touch it, too.

We've brought paper. Dad puts it over the letters and rubs on it with a pencil so the paper goes dark, and the letters show up white.

"You've got parts of other guys' names on there, too," I tell him.

Dad looks at the paper. "Your grandpa won't mind."

"They were probably friends of his anyway," I say.

Dad nods. "Maybe so."

A man and a boy walk past.

"Can we go to the river now, Grandpa?" the boy asks.

"Yes." The man takes the boy's hand. "But button your jacket. It's cold."

My dad stands very still with his head bent.

A bunch of big girls in school uniforms come down the path. Their teacher is with them. They are all carrying more of those little flags.

"Is this wall for the dead soldiers, Miss Gerber?" one of them asks in a loud voice.

"The names are the names of the dead. But the wall is for all of us," the teacher says.

They make a lot of noise and ask a lot of questions and all the time Dad just stands there with his head bowed, and I stand beside him.

The girls stick their flags in the dirt in front of the wall and leave.

Then it's quiet again.

Dad folds the paper that has Grandpa's name on it and
puts it in his wallet. He slides out a picture of me, one of the
yucky ones they took in school. Mom made me wear a tie.
Dad puts the picture on the grass below Grandpa's name.

It blows away.

I get it and put it back and pile some little stones on top.

My face smiles up at me from under the stones.

"Grandpa won't know who I am," I tell Dad.

"I think he will," Dad says.

I move closer to him. "It's sad here."

He puts his hand on my shoulder. "I know. But it's a place of honor. I'm proud that your grandfather's name is on this wall."

"I am, too."

I am.

But I'd rather have my grandpa here, taking me to the
river, telling me to button my jacket because it's cold.
I'd rather have him here.

NOTE

The Vietnam Veterans Memorial honors the men and women of the armed forces of the United States who served in the Vietnam War. On it are listed the names of those who gave their lives and those "missing in action."

The Memorial is located in Washington, D.C. On the long, black wall are more than 58,000 names.

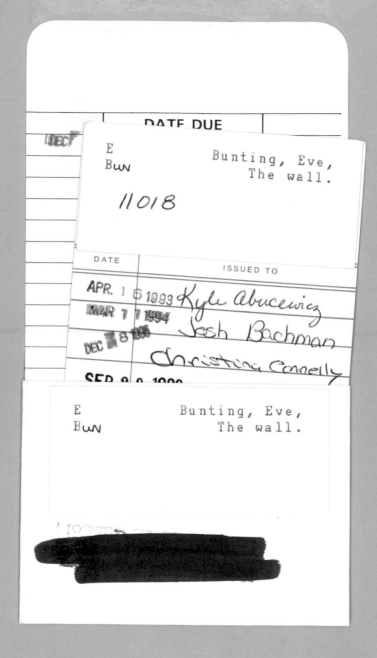